AF306766

Painted Windows

Elia Wilkinson Peattie

Imprint

This book is part of TREDITION CLASSICS

Author: Elia Wilkinson Peattie
Cover design: Buchgut, Berlin – Germany

Publisher: tredition GmbH, Hamburg - Germany
ISBN: 978-3-8424-2709-9

www.tredition.com
www.tredition.de

Copyright:
The content of this book is sourced from the public domain.

The intention of the TREDITION CLASSICS series is to make world literature in the public domain available in printed format. Literary enthusiasts and organizations, such as Project Gutenberg, worldwide have scanned and digitally edited the original texts. tredition has subsequently formatted and redesigned the content into a modern reading layout. Therefore, we cannot guarantee the exact reproduction of the original format of a particular historic edition. Please also note that no modifications have been made to the spelling, therefore it may differ from the orthography used today.

PAINTED WINDOWS

By Elia W. Peattie

Will you come with me into the chamber of memory and lift your eyes to the painted windows where the figures and scenes of childhood appear? Perhaps by looking with kindly eyes at those from out my past, long wished-for visions of your own youth will appear to heal the wounds from which you suffer, and to quiet your stormy and restless heart.

Contents

PAINTED WINDOWS

PAINTED WINDOWS

I. NIGHT

YOUNG people believe very little that they hear about the compensations of growing old, and of living over again in memory the events of the past. Yet there really are these compensations and pleasures, and although they are not so vivid and breathless as the pleasures of youth, they have something delicate and fine about them that must be experienced to be appreciated.

Few of us would exchange our memories for those of others. They have become a part of our personality, and we could not part with them without losing something of ourselves. Neither would we part with our own particular childhood, which, however difficult it may have been at times, seems to each of us more significant than the childhood of any one else. I can run over in my mind certain incidents of my childhood as if they were chapters in a much-loved book, and when I am wakeful at night, or bored by a long journey, or waiting for some one in the railway-station, I take them out and go over them again.

Nor is my book of memories without its illustrations. I can see little villages, and a great city, and forests and planted fields, and familiar faces; and all have this advantage: they are not fixed and without motion, like the pictures in the ordinary book. People are walking up the streets of the village, the trees are tossing, the tall wheat and corn in the fields salute me. I can smell the odour of the gathered hay, and the faces in my dream-book smile at me.

Of all of these memories I like best the one in the pine forest.

I was at that age when children think of their parents as being all-powerful. I could hardly have imagined any circumstances, however adverse, that my father could not have met with his strength and wisdom and skill. All children have such a period of hero-worship, I suppose, when their father stands out from the rest of the world as the best and most powerful man living. So, feeling as I did, I was made happier than I can say when my father decided, because I was looking pale and had a poor appetite, to take me out of school for a while, and carry me with him on a driving trip. We lived in Michigan, where there were, in the days of which I am writing, not many railroads; and when my father, who was attorney for a number of wholesale mercantile firms in Detroit, used to go about the country collecting money due, adjusting claims, and so on, he had no choice but to drive.

And over what roads! Now it was a strip of corduroy, now a piece of well-graded elevation with clay subsoil and gravel surface, now a neglected stretch full of dangerous holes; and worst of all, running through the great forests, long pieces of road from which the stumps had been only partly extracted, and where the sunlight barely penetrated. Here the soaked earth became little less than a quagmire.

But father was too well used to hard journeys to fear them, and I felt that, in going with him, I was safe from all possible harm. The journey had all the allurement of an adventure, for we would not know from day to day where we should eat our meals or sleep at night. So, to provide against trouble, we carried father's old red-and-blue-checked army blankets, a bag of feed for Sheridan, the horse, plenty of bread, bacon, jam, coffee and prepared cream; and we hung pails of pure water and buttermilk from the rear of our buggy.

We had been out two weeks without failing once to eat at a proper table or to sleep in a comfortable bed. Sometimes we put up at the stark-looking hotels that loomed, raw and uninviting, in the larger towns; sometimes we had the pleasure of being welcomed at a little inn, where the host showed us a personal hospitality; but oftener we were forced to make ourselves "paying guests" at some house. We cared nothing whether we slept in the spare rooms of a fine frame "residence" or crept into bed beneath the eaves of the attic in a log cabin. I had begun to feel that our journey would be almost too tame and comfortable, when one night something really happened.

Father lost his bearings. He was hoping to reach the town of Gratiot by nightfall, and he attempted to make a short cut. To do this he turned into a road that wound through a magnificent forest, at first of oak and butternut, ironwood and beech, then of densely growing pines. When we entered the wood it was twilight, but no sooner were we well within the shadow of these sombre trees than we were plunged in darkness, and within half an hour this darkness deepened, so that we could see nothing — not even the horse.

"The sun doesn't get in here the year round," said father, trying his best to guide the horse through the mire. So deep was the mud that it seemed as if it literally sucked at the legs of the horse and the wheels of the buggy, and I began to wonder if we should really be swallowed, and to fear that we had met with a difficulty that even my father could not overcome. I can hardly make plain what a tragic thought that was! The horse began to give out sighs and groans, and in the intervals of his struggles to get on, I could feel him trembling. There was a note of anxiety in father's voice as he called out, with all the authority and cheer he could command, to poor Sheridan. The wind was rising, and the long sobs of the pines made cold shivers run up my spine. My teeth chattered, partly from cold, but more from fright.

"What are we going to do?" I asked, my voice quivering with tears.

"Well, we aren't going to cry, whatever else we do!" answered father, rather sharply. He snatched the lighted lantern from its place on the dashboard and leaped out into the road. I could hear him floundering round in that terrible mire and soothing the horse. The next thing I realised was that the horse was unhitched, that father had — for the first time during our journey — laid the lash across Sheridan's back, and that, with a leap of indignation, the horse had reached the firm ground of the roadside. Father called out to him to stand still, and a moment later I found myself being swung from the buggy into father's arms. He staggered along, plunging and almost falling, and presently I, too, stood beneath the giant pines.

"One journey more," said father, "for our supper, and then we'll bivouac right here."

Now that I was away from the buggy that was so familiar to me, and that seemed like a little movable piece of home, I felt, as I had not felt before, the vastness of the solitude. Above me in the rising wind tossed the tops of the singing trees; about me stretched the soft blackness; and beneath the dense, interlaced branches it was almost as calm and still as in a room. I could see that the clouds were breaking and the stars beginning to come out, and that comforted me a little.

Father was keeping up a stream of cheerful talk.

"Now, sir," he was saying to Sheridan, "stand still while I get this harness off you. I'll tie you and blanket you, and you can lie or stand as you please. Here's your nose-bag, with some good supper in it, and if you don't have drink, it's not my fault. Anyway, it isn't so long since you got a good nip at the creek."

I was watching by the faint light of the lantern, and noticing how unnatural father and Sheridan looked. They seemed to be blocked out in a rude kind of way, like some wooden toys I had at home.

"Here we are," said father, "like Robinson Crusoes. It was hard luck for Robinson, not having his little girl along. He'd have had her to pick up sticks and twigs to make a fire, and that would have been a great help to him."

Father began breaking fallen branches over his knee, and I groped round and filled my arms again and again with little fagots. So after a few minutes we had a fine fire crackling in a place where it could not catch the branches of the trees. Father had scraped the needles of the pines together in such a way that a bare rim of earth was left all around the fire, so that it could not spread along the ground; and presently the coffee-pot was over the fire and bacon was sizzling in the frying-pan. The good, hearty odours came out to mingle with the delicious scent of the pines, and I, setting out our dishes, began to feel a happiness different from anything I had ever known.

Pioneers and wanderers and soldiers have joys of their own—joys of which I had heard often enough, for there had been more stories told than read in our house. But now for the first time I knew what my grandmother and my uncles had meant when they told me about the way they had come into the wilderness, and about the great happiness and freedom of those first days. I, too, felt this freedom, and it seemed to me as if I never again wanted walls to close in on me. All my fear was gone, and I felt wild and glad. I could not believe that I was only a little girl. I felt taller even than my father.

Father's mood was like mine in a way. He had memories to add to his emotion, but then, on the other hand, he lacked the sense of discovery I had, for he had known often such feelings as were coming to me for the first time. When he was a young man he had been a colporteur for the American Bible Society among the Lake Superior Indians, and in that way had earned part of the money for his course at the University of Michigan; afterward he had gone with other gold-seekers to Pike's Peak, and had crossed the plains with oxen, in the company of many other adventurers; then, when President Lincoln called for troops, he had returned to enlist with the Michigan men, and had served more than three years with McClellan and Grant.

So, naturally, there was nothing he did not know about making himself comfortable in the open. He knew all the sorrow and all the joy of the homeless man, and now, as he cooked, he began to sing the old songs — "Marching Through Georgia," and "Bury Me Not on the Lone Prairie," and "In the Prison Cell I Sit." He had been in a Southern prison after the Battle of the Wilderness, and so he knew how to sing that song with particular feeling.

I had heard war stories all my life, though usually father told such tales in a half-joking way, as if to make light of everything he had gone through. But now, as we ate there under the tossing pines, and the wild chorus in the treetops swelled like a rising sea, the spirit of the old days came over him. He was a good "stump speaker," and he knew how to make a story come to life, and never did all his simple natural gifts show themselves better than on this night, when he dwelt on his old campaigns.

For the first time I was to look into the heart of a kindly natured man, forced by terrible necessity to go through the dread experience of war. I gained an idea of the unspeakable homesickness of the man who leaves his family to an unimagined fate, and sacrifices years in the service of his country. I saw that the mere foregoing of roof and bed is an indescribable distress; I learned something of what the palpitant anxiety before a battle must be, and the quaking fear at the first rattle of bullets, and the half-mad rush of determination with which men force valour into their faltering hearts; I was made to know something of the blight of war—the horror of the battlefield, the waste of bounty, the ruin of homes.

Then, rising above this, came stories of devotion, of brotherhood, of service on the long, desolate marches, of courage to the death of those who fought for a cause. I began to see wherein lay the highest joy of the soldier, and of how little account he held himself, if the principle for which he fought could be preserved. I heard for the first time the wonderful words of Lincoln at Gettysburg, and learned to repeat a part of them.

I was only eight, it is true, but emotion has no age, and I understood then as well as I ever could, what heroism and devotion and self-forgetfulness mean. I understood, too, the meaning of the words "our country," and my heart warmed to it, as in the older times the hearts of boys and girls warmed to the name of their king. The new knowledge was so beautiful that I thought then, and I think now, that nothing could have served as so fit an accompaniment to it as the shouting of those pines. They sang like heroes, and in their swaying gave me fleeting glimpses of the stars, unbelievably brilliant in the dusky purple sky, and half-obscured now and then by drifting clouds.

By and by we lay down, not far apart, each rolled in an army blanket, frayed with service. Our feet were to the fire—for it was so that soldiers lay, my father said—and our heads rested on mounds of pine-needles.

Sometimes in the night I felt my father's hand resting lightly on my shoulders to see that I was covered, but in my dreams he ceased to be my father and became my comrade, and I was a drummer boy,—I had seen the play, "The Drummer Boy of the Rappahannock,"—marching forward, with set teeth, in the face of battle.

Whatever could redeem war and make it glorious seemed to flood my soul. All that was highest, all that was noble in that dreadful conflict came to me in my sleep—to me, the child who had been born when my father was at "the front." I had a strange baptism of the spirit. I discovered sorrow and courage, singing trees and stars. I was never again to think that the fireside and fireside thoughts made up the whole of life.

My father lies with other soldiers by the Pacific; the forest sings no more; the old army blankets have disappeared; the memories of the terrible war are fading,—happily fading,—but they all live again, sometimes, in my memory, and I am once more a child, with thoughts as proud and fierce and beautiful as Valkyries.

II. SOLITUDE

AMONG the pictures that I see when I look back into the past, is the one where I, a sullen, egotistic person nine years old, stood quite alone in the world. To be sure, there were father and mother in the house, and there were the other children, and not one among them knew I was alone. The world certainly would not have regarded me as friendless or orphaned. There was nothing in my mere appearance, as I started away to school in my clean ginghams, with my well-brushed hair, and embroidered school-bag, to lead any one to suppose that I was a castaway. Yet I was—I had discovered this fact, hidden though it might be from others.

I was no longer loved. Father and mother loved the other children; but not me. I might come home at night, fairly bursting with important news about what had happened in class or among my friends, and try to relate my little histories. But did mother listen? Not at all. She would nod like a mandarin while I talked, or go on turning the leaves of her book, or writing her letter. What I said was of no importance to her.

Father was even less interested. He frankly told me to keep still, and went on with the accounts in which he was so absurdly interested, or examined "papers"—stupid-looking things done on legal cap, which he brought home with him from the office. No one kissed me when I started away in the morning; no one kissed me when I came home at night. I went to bed unkissed. I felt myself to be a lonely and misunderstood child—perhaps even an adopted one.

Why, I knew a little girl who, when she went up to her room at night, found the bedclothes turned back, and the shade drawn, and a screen placed so as to keep off drafts. And her mother brushed her hair twenty minutes by the clock each night, to make it glossy; and then she sat by her bed and sang softly till the girl fell asleep.

I not only had to open my own bed, but the beds for the other children, and although I sometimes felt my mother's hand tucking in the bedclothes round me, she never stooped and kissed me on the brow and said, "Bless you, my child." No one, in all my experience, had said, "Bless you, my child." When the girl I have spoken of came into the room, her mother reached out her arms and said, before everybody, "Here comes my dear little girl." When I came into a room, I was usually told to do something for somebody. It was "Please see if the fire needs more wood," or "Let the cat in, please," or "I'd like you to weed the pansy bed before supper-time."

In these circumstances, life hardly seemed worth living. I decided that I had made a mistake in choosing my family. It did not appreciate me, and it failed to make my young life glad. I knew my young life ought to be glad. And it was not. It was drab, as drab as Toot's old rain-coat.

Toot was "our coloured boy." That is the way we described him. Father had brought him home from the war, and had sent him to school, and then apprenticed him to a miller. Toot did "chores" for his board and clothes, but was soon to be his own man, and to be paid money by the miller, and to marry Tulula Darthula Jones, a nice coloured girl who lived with the Cutlers.

The time had been when Toot had been my self-appointed slave. Almost my first recollections were of his carrying me out to see the train pass, and saying, "Toot, toot!" in imitation of the locomotive; so, although he had rather a splendid name, I called him "Toot," and the whole town followed my example. Yes, the time had been when Toot saw me safe to school, and slipped little red apples into my pocket, and took me out while he milked the cow, and told me stories and sang me plantation songs. Now, when he passed, he only nodded. When I spoke to him about his not giving me any more apples, he said:

"Ah reckon they're your pa's apples, missy. Why, fo' goodness' sake, don' yo' he'p yo'se'f?"

But I did not want to help myself. I wanted to be helped — not because I was lazy, but because I wanted to be adored. I was really a sort of fairy princess, — misplaced, of course, in a stupid republic, — and I wanted life conducted on a fairy-princess basis. It was a game I wished to play, but it was one I could not play alone, and not a soul could I find who seemed inclined to play it with me.

Well, things went from bad to worse. I decided that if mother no longer loved me, I would no longer tell her things. So I did not. I got a hundred in spelling for twelve days running, and did not tell her! I broke Edna Grantham's mother's water-pitcher, and kept the fact a secret. The secret was, indeed, as sharp-edged as the pieces of the broken pitcher had been; I cried under the bedclothes, thinking how sorry Mrs. Grantham had been, and that mother really ought to know. Only what was the use? I no longer looked to her to help me out of my troubles.

I had no need now to have father and mother tell me to hurry up and finish my chatter, for I kept all that happened to myself. I had a new "intimate friend," and did not so much as mention her. I wrote a poem and showed it to my teacher, but not to my uninterested parents. And when I climbed the stairs at night to my room, I swelled with loneliness and anguish and resentment, and the hot tears came to my eyes as I heard father and mother laughing and talking together and paying no attention to my misery. I could hear Toot, who used to be making all sorts of little presents for me, whistling as he brought in the wood and water, and then "cleaned up" to go to see his Tulula, with never a thought of me. And I said to myself that the best thing I could do was to grow up and get away from a place where I was no longer wanted.

No one noticed my sufferings further than sometimes to say impatiently, "What makes you act so strange, child?" And to that, of course, I answered nothing, for what I had to say would not, I felt, be understood.

One morning in June I left home with my resentment burning fiercely within me. I had not cared for the things we had for breakfast, for I was half-ill with fretting and with the closeness of the day, but my lack of appetite had been passed by with the remark that any one was likely not to have an appetite on such a close day. But I was so languid, and so averse to taking up the usual round of things, that I begged mother to let me stay at home. She shook her head decidedly.

"You've been out of school too many days already this term," she said. "Run along now, or you'll be late!"

"Please—" I began, for my head really was whirling, although, quite as much, perhaps, from my perversity as from any other cause. Mother turned on me one of her "last-word" glances.

"Go to school without another word," she said, quietly.

I knew that quiet tone, and I went. And now I was sure that all was over between my parents and myself. I began to wonder if I need really wait till I was grown up before leaving home. So miserably absorbed was I in thinking of this, and in pitying myself with a consuming pity, that everything at school seemed to pass like the shadow of a dream. I blundered in whatever I tried to do, was sharply scolded for not hearing the teacher until she had spoken my name three times, and was holding on to myself desperately in my effort to keep back a flood of tears, when I became aware that something was happening.

There suddenly was a perfect silence in the room—the sort of silence that makes the heart beat too fast. The mist swimming before me did not, I perceived, come from my own eyes, but from the changing colour of the air, the usual transparency of which was being tinged with yellow. The sultriness of the day was deepening, and seemed to carry a threat with it.

"Something is going to happen," thought I, and over the whole room spread the same conviction. Electric currents seemed to snap from one consciousness to another. We dropped our books, and turned our eyes toward the western windows, to look upon a changed world. It was as if we peered through yellow glass. In the sky soft-looking, tawny clouds came tumbling along like playful cats—or tigers. A moment later we saw that they were not playful, but angry; they stretched out claws, and snarled as they did so. One claw reached the tall chimneys of the schoolhouse, another tapped at the cupola, one was thrust through the wall near where I sat.

Then it grew black, and there was a bellowing all about us, so that the commands of the teacher and the screams of the children barely could be heard. I knew little or nothing. My shoulder was stinging, something had hit me on the side of the head, my eyes were full of dust and mortar, and my feet were carrying me with the others along the corridor, down the two flights of wide stairs. I do not think we pushed each other or were reckless. My recollection is only of many shadowy figures flying on with sure feet out of the building that seemed to be falling in upon us.

Presently we were out on the landing before the door, with one more flight of steps before us, that reached to the street. Something so strong that it might not be denied gathered me up in invisible arms, whirled me round once or twice and dropped me, not ungently, in the middle of the road. And then, as I struggled to my knees and, wiping the dust from my eyes, looked up, I saw dozens of others being lifted in the same way, and blown off into the yard or the street. The larger ones were trying to hold on to the smaller, and the teachers were endeavouring to keep the children from going out of the building, but their efforts were of no avail. The children came on, and were blown about like leaves.

Then I saw what looked like a high yellow wall advancing upon me—a roaring and fearsome mass of driven dust, sticks, debris. It came over me that my own home might be there, in strips and fragments, to beat me down and kill me; and with the thought came a swift little vision out of my geography of the Arabs in a sandstorm on the desert. I gathered up my fluttering dress skirt, held it tight about my head, and lay flat upon the ground.

It seemed as if a long time passed, a time in which I knew very little except that I was fighting for my breath as I never had fought for anything. There were more hurts and bruises now, but they did not matter. Just to draw my own breath in my own way seemed to be the only thing in the world that was of any account. And then there was a shaft of flame, an earsplitting roar, and the rain was upon us in sheets, in streams, in visible rivers.

I imagined that it would last a long time, and wondered in a daze how I could get home in a rain like that—for I should have to face it. I could see that in a few seconds the gutters had begun to race, the road where I lay was a stream, and then—then the rain ceased. Never was anything so astonishing. The sky came out blue, tattered rags of cloud raced across it, and I had time to conclude that, whipped and almost breathless though I was, I was still alive.

And then I saw a curious sight. Down the street in every direction came rushing hatless men and women. Here and there a wild-eyed horse was being lashed along. All the town was coming. They were in their work clothes, in their slippers, in their wrappers—they were in anything and everything. Some of them sobbed as they ran, some called aloud names that I knew. They were fathers and mothers looking for their children.

And who was that—that woman with a white face, with hair falling about her shoulders, where it had fallen as she ran—that woman whose breath came between her teeth strangely and who called my name over and over, bleatingly, as a mother sheep calls its lamb? At first I did not recognise her, and then, at last, I knew. And that creature with the rolling eyes and the curious ash-coloured face who, mumbling something over and over in his throat, came for me, and snatched me up and wiped my face free of mud, and felt of me here and there with trembling hands—who was he?

And breaking out of the crowd of men who had come running from the street of stores and offices, was another strange being, with a sort of battle light in his eyes, who, seeing me, gathered me to him and bore me away toward home. Looking back, I could see the woman I knew following, leaning on the arm of the boy with the rolling eyes, whose eyes had ceased to roll, and who was quite recognisable now as Toot.

A happiness that was almost as terrible as sorrow welled up in my heart. I did not weep, or laugh, or talk. All I had experienced had carried me beyond mere excitement into exultation. I exulted in life, in love. My conceit and sulkiness died in that storm, as did many another thing. I was alive. I was loved. I said it over and over to myself silently, in "my heart's deep core," while mother washed me with trembling hands in my own dear room, bound up my hurts, braided my hair, and put me, in a fresh night-dress, into my bed. I do not recall that we talked to each other, but in every caress of her hands as she worked I felt the unspoken assurances of a love such as I had not dreamed of.

Father had gone running back to the school to see if he could be of any assistance to his neighbours, and had taken Toot with him, but they were back presently to say that beyond a few sharp injuries and broken bones, no harm had been done to the children. It was considered miraculous that no one had been killed or seriously injured, and I noticed that father's voice trembled as he told of it, and that mother could not answer, and that Toot sobbed like a big silly boy.

Then as we talked together, behold, a second storm was upon us—a sharp black blast of wind and rain, not terrifying, like the other, but with an "I've-come-to-spend-the-day" sort of aspect.

But no one seemed to mind very much. I was carried down to the sitting-room. Toot busied himself coming and going on this errand and on that, fastening the doors, closing the windows, running out to see to the animals, and coming back again. Father and mother set the table. They kept close together; and now and then they looked over at me, without saying anything, but with shining eyes.

The storm died down to a quiet rain. From the roof of the porch the drops fell in silver strings, like beads. Then the sun came out and turned them into shining crystal. The birds began to sing again, and when we threw open the windows delicious odours of fresh earth and flowering shrub greeted us. Mother began to sing as she worked. And I sank softly to sleep, thrilled with the marvels of the world—not of the tempest, but of the peace.

The sweet familiarity of the faces and the walls and the furniture and the garden was like a blessing. There was not a chair there that I would have exchanged for any other chair—not a tree that I would have parted with—not a custom of that simple, busy place that I would have changed. I knew now all my stupidity—and my good fortune.

III. FRIENDSHIP

WHEN I look back upon the village where I lived as a child, I cannot remember that there were any divisions in our society. This group went to the Congregational church, and that to the Presbyterian, but each family felt itself to be as good as any other, and even if, ordinarily, some of them withdrew themselves in mild exclusiveness, on all occasions of public celebration, or when in trouble, we stood together in the pleasantest and most unaffected democracy.

There were only the "Bad Madigans" outside the pale.

The facts about the Bad Madigans were, no doubt, serious enough, but the fiction was even more appalling. As to facts, the father drank, the mother followed suit, the appearance of the house—a ramshackle old place beyond the fair-grounds—was a scandal; the children could not be got to go to school for any length of time, and, when they were there, each class in which they were put felt itself to be in disgrace, and the dislike focused upon the intruders, sent them, sullen and hateful, back to their lair. And, indeed, the Madigan house seemed little more than a lair. It had been rather a fine house once, and had been built for the occupancy of the man who owned the fairgrounds; but he choosing finally to live in the village, had permitted the house to fall into decay, until only a family with no sense of order or self-respect would think of occupying it.

When there occurred one of the rare burglaries in the village, when anything was missing from a clothes-line, or a calf or pig disappeared, it was generally laid to the Madigans. Unaccounted-for fires were supposed to be their doing; they were accorded responsibility for vicious practical jokes; and it was generally felt that before we were through with them they would commit some blood-curdling crime.

When, as sometimes happened, I had met one of the Bad Madigans on the road, or down on the village street, my heart had beaten as if I was face to face with a company of banditti; but I cannot say that this excitement was caused by aversion alone. The truth was, the Bad Madigans fascinated me. They stood out from all the others, proudly and disdainfully like Robin Hood and his band, and I could not get over the idea that they said: "Fetch me yonder bow!" to each other; or, "Go slaughter me a ten-tined buck!" I felt that they were fortunate in not being held down to hours like the rest of us. Out of bed at six-thirty, at table by seven, tidying bedroom at seven-thirty, dusting sitting-room at eight, on way to school at eight-thirty, was not for "the likes of them!" Only we, slaves of respectability and of an inordinate appetite for order, suffered such monotony and drabness to rule. I knew the Madigan boys could go fishing whenever they pleased, that the Madigan girls picked the blackberries before any one else could get out to them, that every member of the family could pack up and go picnicking for days at a time, and that any stray horse was likely to be ridden bareback, within an inch of its life, by the younger members of the family.

Only once however, did I have a chance to meet one of these modern Visigoths face to face, and the feelings aroused by that incident remained the darling secret of my youth. I dared tell no one, and I longed, yet feared, to have the experience repeated. But it never was! It happened in this way:

On a certain Sunday afternoon in May, my father and mother and I went to Emmons' Woods. To reach Emmons' Woods, you went out the back door, past the pump and the currant bushes, then down the path to the chicken-houses, and so on, by way of the woodpile, to the south gate. After that, you went west toward the clover meadows, past the house where the Crazy Lady lived—here, if you were alone, you ran—and then, reaching the verge of the woods, you took your choice of climbing a seven-rail fence or of walking a quarter of a mile till you came to the bars. The latter was much better for the lace on a Sunday petticoat.

Once in Emmons' Woods, there was enchantment. An eagle might come—or a blue heron. There had been bears in Emmons' Woods—bears with rolling eyes and red mouths from which their tongues lolled. There was one place for pinky trillium, and another for gentians; one for tawny adders' tongues, and another for yellow Dutchman's breeches. In the sap-starting season, the maples dripped their luscious sap into little wooden cups; later, partridges nested in the sun-burned grass. There was no lake or river, but there was a pond, swarming with a vivacious population, and on the hard-baked clay of the pond beach the green beetles aired their splendid changeable silks and sandpipers hopped ridiculously.

It was, curiously enough, easier to run than to walk in Emmons' Woods, and even more natural to dance than to run. One became acquainted with squirrels, established intimacies with chipmunks, and was on some sort of civil relation with blackbirds. And, oh, the tossing green of the young willows, where the lilac distance melted into the pale blue of the sky! And, oh, the budding of the maples and the fringing of the oaks; and, oh, the blossoming of the tulip trees and the garnering of the chestnuts! And then, the wriggling things in the grass; the procession of ants; the coquetries of the robins; and the Beyond, deepening, deepening into the forest where it was safe only for the woodsmen to go.

On this particular Sunday one of us was requested not to squeal and run about, and to remember that we wore our best shoes and need not mess them unnecessarily. It was hard to be reminded just when the dance was getting into my feet, but I tried to have Sunday manners, and went along in the still woods, wondering why the purple colours disappeared as we came on and what had been distance became nearness. There was a beautiful, aching vagueness over everything, and it was not strange that father, who had stretched himself on the moss, and mother, who was reading Godey's Ladies' Book, should presently both of them be nodding. So, that being a well-established fact—I established it by hanging over them and staring at their eyelids—it seemed a good time for me to let the dance out of my toes. Still careful of my fresh linen frock, and remembering about the best shoes, I went on, demurely, down the green alleys of the wood. Now I stepped on patches of sunshine, now in pools of shadow. I thought of how naughty I was to run away like this, and of what a mistake people made who said I was a good, quiet, child. I knew that I looked sad and prim, but I really hated my sadness and primness and goodness, and longed to let out all the interesting, wild, naughty thoughts there were in me. I wanted to act as if I were bewitched, and to tear up vines and wind them about me, to shriek to the echoes, and to scold back at the squirrels. I wanted to take off my clothes and rush into the pond, and swim like a fish, or wriggle like a pollywog. I wanted to climb trees and drop from them; and, most of all—oh, with what long-ing—did I wish to lift myself above the earth and fly into the bland blue air!

I came to a hollow where there was a wonderful greenness over everything, and I said to myself that I would be bewitched at last. I would dance and whirl and call till, perhaps, some kind of a crea-ture as wild and wicked and wonderful as I, would come out of the woods and join me. So I forgot about the fresh linen frock, and wreathed myself with wild grape-vine; I cared nothing for my fresh braids and wound trillium in my hair; and I ceased to remember my new shoes, and whirled around and around in the leafy mould, singing and shouting.

I grew madder and madder. I seemed not to be myself at all, but some sort of a wood creature; and just when the trees were looking larger than ever they did before, and the sky higher up, a girl came running down from a sort of embankment where a tornado had made a path for itself and had hurled some great chestnuts and oaks in a tumbled mass. The girl came leaping down the steep sides of this place, her arms outspread, her feet bare, her dress no more than a rag the colour of the tree-trunks. She had on a torn green jacket, which made her seem more than ever like some one who had just stepped out of a hollow tree, and, to my unspeakable happi-ness, she joined me in my dance.

I shall never forget how beautiful she was, with her wild tangle of dark hair, and her deep blue eyes and ripe lips. Her cheeks were flaming red, and her limbs strong and brown. She did not merely shout and sing; she whistled, and made calls like the birds, and cawed like a crow, and chittered like a squirrel, and around and around the two of us danced, crazy as dervishes with the beauty of the spring and the joy of being free.

By and by we were so tired we had to stop, and then we sat down panting and looked at each other. At that we laughed, long and foolishly, but, after a time, it occurred to us that we had many ques-tions to ask.

"How did you get here?" I asked the girl.

"I was walking my lone," she said, speaking her words as if there was a rich thick quality to them, "and I heard you screeling."

"Won't you get lost, alone like that?"

"I can't get lost," she sighed. "I 'd like to, but I can't."

"Where do you live?"

"Beyant the fair-grounds."

"You're not—not Norah Madigan?"

She leaned back and clasped her hands behind her head. Then she smiled at me teasingly.

"I am that," she said, showing her perfect teeth.

I caught my breath with a sharp gasp. Ought I to turn back to my parents? Had I been so naughty that I had called the naughtiest girl in the whole county out to me?

But I could not bring myself to leave her. She was leaning forward and looking at me now with mocking eyes.

"Are you afraid?" she demanded.

"Afraid of what?" I asked, knowing quite well what she meant.

"Of me?" she retorted.

At that second an agreeable truth overtook me. I leaned forward, too, and put my hand on hers.

"Why, I like you!" I cried. She began laughing again, but this time there was no mockery in it. She ran her fingers over the embroidery on my linen frock, she examined the lace on my petticoat, looked at the bows on my shoes, and played delicately with the locket dangling from the slender chain around my neck.

"Do you know—other girls?" she almost whispered.

I nodded. "Lots and lots of 'em," I said. "Don't you?"

She shook her head in wistful denial.

"Us Madigans," she said, "keeps to ourselves." She said it so haughtily that for a moment I was almost persuaded into thinking that they lived their solitary lives from choice. But, glancing up at her, I saw a blush that covered her face, and there were tears in her eyes.

"Well, anyway," said I quickly, "we know each other."

"Yes," she cried, "we do that!"

She got up, then, and ran to a great tree from which a stout grape-vine was swinging, and pulling at it with her strong arms, she soon had it made into a practical swing.

"Come!" she called—"come, let's swing together!"

She helped me to balance myself on the rope-like vine, and, placing her feet outside of mine, showed me how to "work up" till we were sweeping with a fine momentum through the air. We shrieked with excitement, and urged each other on to more and more frantic exertions. We were like two birds, but to birds flying is no novelty. With us it was, which made us happier than birds. But I, for my part, was no more delighted with my swift flights through the air than I was with the shining eyes and flashing teeth of the girl opposite me. I liked her strength, and the way in which her body bent and swayed. Once more, she seemed like a wood-child—a wild, mad, gay creature from the tree. I felt as if I had drawn a playmate from elf-land, and I liked her a thousand times better than those proper little girls who came to see me of a Saturday afternoon.

Well, there we were, rocking and screaming, and telling each other that we were hawks, and that we were flying high over the world, when the anxious and austere voice of my mother broke upon our ears. We tried to stop, but that was not such an easy matter to do, and as we twisted and writhed, to bring our grape-vine swing to a standstill, there was a slow rending and breaking which struck terror to our souls.

"Jump!" commanded Norah—"jump! the vine's breaking!" We leaped at the same moment, she safely. My foot caught in a stout tendril, and I fell headlong, scraping my forehead on the ground and tearing a triangular rent in the pretty, new frock. Mother came running forward, and the expression on her face was far from being the one I liked to see.

"What have you been doing?" she demanded. "I thought you were getting old enough and sensible enough to take care of yourself!"

I must have been a depressing sight, viewed with the eyes of a careful mother. Blood and mould mingled on my face, my dress needed a laundress as badly as a dress could, and my shoes were scratched and muddy.

"And who is this girl?" asked mother. I had become conscious that Norah was at my feet, wiping off my shoes with her queer little brown frock.

"It's a new friend of mine," gasped I, beginning to see that I must lose her, and hoping the lump in my throat wouldn't get any bigger than it was.

"What is her name?" asked mother. I had no time to answer. The girl did that.

"I'm Norah Madigan," she said. Her tone was respectful, and, maybe, sad. At any rate, it had a curious sound.

"Norah Mad-i-gan?" asked mother doubtfully, stringing out the word.

"Yessum," said a low voice. "Goodbye, mum."

"Oh, Norah!" cried I, a strange pain stabbing my heart. "Come to see me —"

But my mother's voice broke in, firm and kind.

"Good-bye, Norah," said she.

I saw Norah turn and run up among the trees, almost as swiftly and silently as a hare. Once, she turned to look back. I was watching, and caught the chance to wave my hand to her.

"Come!" commanded mother, and we went back to where father was sitting.

"What do you think!" said mother. "I found the child playing with one of the Bad Madigans. Isn't she a sight!"

The lump in my throat swelled to a terrible size; something buzzed in my ears, and I heard some one weeping. For a second or two I didn't realise that it was myself.

"Well, never mind, dear," said mother's voice soothingly. "The frock will wash, and the tear will mend, and the shoes will black. Yes, and the scratches will heal."

"It isn't that," I sobbed. "Oh, oh, it isn't that!"

"What is it, then, for goodness sake?" asked mother.

But I would not tell. I could not tell. How could I say that the daughter of the Bad Madigans was the first real and satisfying playmate I had ever had?

IV. FAME

AS I remember the boys and girls who grew up with me, I think of them as artists, or actors, or travellers, or rich merchants. Each of us, by the time we were half through grammar school, had selected a career. So far as I recollect, this career had very little to do with our abilities. We merely chose something that suited us. Our energy and our vanity crystallised into particular shapes. There was a sort of religion abroad in the West at that time that a person could do almost anything he set out to do. The older people, as well as the children, had an idea that the world was theirs—they all were Monte Cristos in that respect.

As for me, I had decided to be an orator.

At the time of making this decision, I was nine years of age, decidedly thin and long drawn out, with two brown braids down my back, and a terrific shyness which I occasionally overcame with such a magnificent splurge that those who were not acquainted with my peculiarities probably thought me a shamefully assertive child.

I based my oratorical aspirations upon my having taken the prize a number of times in Sunday-school for learning the most New Testament verses, and upon the fact that I always could make myself heard to the farthest corner of the room. I also felt that I had a great message to deliver to the world when I got around it, though in this, I was in no way different from several of my friends. I had noticed a number of things in the world that were not quite right, and which I thought needed attention, and I believed that if I were quite good and studied elocution, in a little while I should be able to set my part of the world right, and perhaps even extend my influence to adjoining districts.

Meantime I practised terrible vocal exercises, chiefly consisting of a raucous "caw" something like a crow's favourite remark, and advocated by my teacher in elocution for no reason that I can now remember; and I stood before the glass for hours at a time making grimaces so as to acquire the "actor's face," till my frightened little sisters implored me to turn back into myself again.

It was a great day for me when I was asked to participate in the Harvest Home Festival at our church on Thanksgiving Day. I looked upon it as the beginning of my career, and bought crimping papers so that my hair could be properly fluted. Of course, I wanted a new dress for the occasion, and I spent several days in planning the kind of a one I thought best suited to such a memorable event. I even picked out the particular lace pattern I wanted for the ruffles. This was before I submitted the proposition to Mother, however. When I told her about it she said she could see no use in getting a new dress and going to all the trouble of making it when my white one with the green harps was perfectly good.

This was such an unusual dress and had gone through so many vicissitudes, that I really was devotedly attached to it. It had, in the beginning, belonged to my Aunt Bess, and in the days of its first glory had been a sheer Irish linen lawn, with tiny green harps on it at agreeable intervals. But in the course of time, it had to be sent to the wash-tub, and then, behold, all the little lovely harps followed the example of the harp that "once through Tara's hall the soul of music shed," and disappeared! Only vague, dirty, yellow reminders of their beauty remained, not to decorate, but to disfigure the fine fabric.

Aunt Bess, naturally enough, felt irritated, and she gave the goods to mother, saying that she might be able to boil the yellow stains out of it and make me a dress. I had gone about many a time, like love amid the ruins, in the fragments of Aunt Bess's splendour, and I was not happy in the thought of dangling these dimmed reminders of Ireland's past around with me. But mother said she thought I'd have a really truly white Sunday best dress out of it by the time she was through with it. So she prepared a strong solution of sodium and things, and boiled the breadths, and every little green harp came dancing back as if awaiting the hand of a new Dublin poet. The green of them was even more charming than it had been at first, and I, as happy as if I had acquired the golden harp for which I then vaguely longed, went to Sunday-school all that summer in this miraculous dress of now-you-see-them and-now-you-don't, and became so used to being asked if I were Irish that my heart exulted when I found that I might—fractionally— claim to be, and that one of the Fenian martyrs had been an ancestor. For a year, even, after that discovery of the Fenian martyr, ancestors were a favorite study of mine.

Well, though the dress became something more than familiar to the eyes of my associates, I was so attached to it that I felt no objection to wearing it on the great occasion; and, that being settled, all that remained was to select the piece which was to reveal my talents to a hitherto unappreciative—or, perhaps I should say, unsuspecting—group of friends and relatives. It seemed to me that I knew better than my teacher (who had agreed to select the pieces for her pupils) possibly could what sort of a thing best represented my talents, and so, after some thought, I selected "Antony and Cleopatra," and as I lagged along the too-familiar road to school, avoiding the companionship of my acquaintances, I repeated:

> I am dying, Egypt, dying! Ebbs the crimson life-tide fast, And the dark Plutonian shadows Gather on the evening blast.

Sometimes I grew so impassioned, so heedless of all save my mimic sorrow and the swing of the purple lines, that I could not bring myself to modify my voice, and the passers-by heard my shrill tones vibrating with:

> As for thee, star-eyed Egyptian! Glorious sorceress of the Nile! Light the path to Stygian horrors With the splendour of thy smile.

I wiped dishes to the rhythm of such phrases as "scarred and veteran legions," and laced my shoes to the music of "Though no glittering guards surround me."

Confident that no one could fail to see the beauty of these lines, or the propriety of the identification of myself with Antony, I called upon my Sunday-school teacher, Miss Goss, to report. I never had thought of Miss Goss as a blithe spirit. She was associated in my mind with numerous solemn occasions, and I was surprised to find that on this day she unexpectedly developed a trait of breaking into nervous laughter. I had got as far as "Should the base plebeian rabble—" when Miss Goss broke down in what I could not but regard as a fit of giggles, and I ceased abruptly.

She pulled herself together after a moment or two, and said if I would follow her to the library she thought she could find something—here she hesitated, to conclude with, "more within the understanding of the other children." I saw that she thought my feelings were hurt, and as I passed a mirror I feared she had some reason to think so. My face was uncommonly flushed, and a look of indignation had crept, somehow, even into my braids, which, having been plaited too tightly, stuck out in crooks and kinks from the side of my head. Incidentally, I was horrified to notice how thin I was—thin, even for a dying Antony—and my frock was so outgrown that it hardly covered my knees. "Ridiculous!" I said under my breath, as I confronted this miserable figure—so shamefully insignificant for the vicarious emotions which it had been housing. "Ridiculous!"

I hated Miss Goss, and must have shown it in my stony stare, for she put her arm around me and said it was a pity I had been to all the trouble to learn a poem which was—well, a trifle too—too old—but that she hoped to find something equally "pretty" for me to speak. At the use of that adjective in connection with William Lytle's lines, I wrenched away from her grasp and stood in what I was pleased to think a haughty calm, awaiting her directions.

She took from the shelves a little volume of Whittier, bound in calf, handling it as tenderly as if it were a priceless possession. Some pressed violets dropped out as she opened it, and she replaced them with devotional fingers. After some time she decided upon a lyric lament entitled "Eva." I was asked to run over the verses, and found them remarkably easy to learn; fatally impossible to forget. I presently arose and with an impish betrayal of the poverty of rhyme and the plethora of sentiment, repeated the thing relentlessly.

> O for faith like thine, sweet Eva, Lighting all the solemn reevah [river], And the blessings of the poor, Wafting to the heavenly shoor [shore].

"I do think," said Miss Goss gently, "that if you tried, my child, you might manage the rhymes just a little better."

"But if you're born in Michigan," I protested, "how can you possibly make 'Eva' rhyme with 'never' and 'believer'?"

"Perhaps it is a little hard," Miss Goss agreed, and still clinging to her Whittier, she exhumed "The Pumpkin," which she thought precisely fitted for our Harvest Home festival. This was quite another thing from "Eva," and I saw that only hours of study would fix it in my mind. I went to my home, therefore, with "The Pumpkin" delicately transcribed in Miss Goss's running hand, and I tried to get some comfort from the foreign allusions glittering through Whittier's kindly verse. As the days went by I came to have a certain fondness for those homely lines:

> O—fruit loved of boyhood!—the old days recalling, When
> wood grapes were purpling and brown nuts were falling!
> When wild, ugly faces we carved in the skin, Glaring out
> through the dark with a candle within! When we laughed
> round the corn-heap, with hearts all in tune, Our chair a
> broad pumpkin—our lantern the moon, Telling tales of the
> fairy who travelled like steam In a pumpkin-shell coach, with
> two rats for her team!

On all sides this poem was considered very fitting, and I went to the festival with that comfortable feeling one has when one is moving with the majority and is wearing one's best clothes.

I sat rigid with expectancy while my schoolmates spoke their "pieces" and sang their songs. With frozen faces they faced each other in dialogues, lost their quavering voices, and stumbled down the stairs in their anguish of spirit. I pitied them, and thought how lucky it was that my memory never failed me, and that my voice carried so well that I could arouse even old Elder Waite from his slumbers.

Then my turn came. My crimps were beautiful; the green harps danced on my freshly-ironed frock, and I had on my new chain and locket. I relied upon a sort of mechanism in me to say: O greenly and fair in the lands of the sun, The vines of the gourd and the rich melon run.

In this seemly manner Whittier's ode to the pumpkin began. I meant to go on to verses which I knew would delight my audience — to references to the "crook-necks" ripening under the September sun; and to Thanksgiving gatherings at which all smiled at the reunion of friends and the bounty of the board.

> What moistens the lip and brightens the eye! What calls back the past like the rich pumpkin pie!

I was sure these lines would meet with approval, and having "come down to the popular taste," I was prepared to do my best to please.

After a few seconds, when the golden pumpkins that lined the stage had ceased to dance before my eyes, I thought I ought to begin to "get hold of my audience." Of course, my memory would be giving me the right words, and my facile tongue running along reliably, but I wished to demonstrate that "ability" which was to bring me favour and fame. I listened to my own words and was shivered into silence. I was talking about "dark Plutonian shadows"; I was begging "Egypt" to let her arms enfold me — I was, indeed, in the very thick of the forbidden poem. I could hear my thin, aspiring voice reaching out over that paralysed audience with:

> Though my scarred and veteran legions Bear their eagles high no more; And my wrecked and scattered galleys Strew dark Actium's fatal shore.

My tongue seemed frozen, or some kind of a ratchet at the base of it had got out of order. For a moment — a moment can be the little sister of eternity — I could say nothing. Then I found myself in the clutches of the instinct for self-preservation. I felt it in me to stop the giggles of the girls on the front seat; to take the patronising smiles out of the tolerant eyes of the grown people. Maybe my voice lost something of its piping insistence and was touched with genuine feeling; perhaps some faint, faint spark of the divine fire which I longed to fan into a flame did flicker in me for that one time. I had the indescribable happiness of seeing the smiles die on the faces of my elders, and of hearing the giggles of my friends cease.

I went to my seat amid what I was pleased to consider "thunders of applause," and by way of acknowledgment, I spoke, with chastened propriety, Whittier's ode to the pumpkin.

I cannot remember whether or not I was scolded. I'm afraid, afterward, some people still laughed. As for me, oddly enough, my oratorical aspirations died. I decided there were other careers better fitted to one of my physique. So I had to go to the trouble of finding another career; but just what it was I have forgotten.

V. REMORSE

IT is extraordinary, when you come to think of it, how very few days, out of all the thousands that have passed, lift their heads from the grey plain of the forgotten—like bowlders in a level stretch of country. It is not alone the unimportant ones that are forgotten; but, according to one's elders, many important ones have left no mark in the memory. It seems to me, as I think it over, that it was the days that affected the emotions that dwell with me, and I suppose all of us must be the same in this respect.

Among those which I am never to forget is the day when Aunt Cordelia came to visit us—my mother's aunt, she was—and when I discovered evil, and tried to understand what the use of it was.

Great-aunt Cordelia was, as I often and often had been told, not only much travelled, rich and handsome, but good also. She was, indeed, an important personage in her own city, and it seemed to be regarded as an evidence of unusual family fealty that she should go about, now and then, briefly visiting all of her kinfolk to see how they fared in the world. I ought to have looked forward to meeting her, but this, for some perverse reason, I did not do. I wished I might run away and hide somewhere till her visit was over. It annoyed me to have to clean up the play-room on her account, and to help polish the silver, and to comb out the fringe of the tea napkins. I liked to help in these tasks ordinarily, but to do it for the purpose of coming up to a visiting and probably, a condescending—goddess, somehow made me cross.

Among other hardships, I had to take care of my little sister Julie all day. I loved Julie. She had soft golden-brown curls fuzzing around on her head, and mischievous brown eyes—warm, extra-human eyes. There was a place in the back of her neck, just below the point of her curls, which it was a privilege to kiss; and though she could not yet talk, she had a throaty, beautiful little exclamation, which cannot be spelled any more than a bird note, with which she greeted all the things she liked—a flower, or a toy, or mother. But loving Julie as she sat in mother's lap, and having to care for her all of a shining Saturday, were two quite different things. As the hours wore along I became bored with looking at the golden curls of my baby sister; I had no inclination to kiss the "honey-spot" in the back of her neck; and when she fretted from heat and teething and my perfunctory care, I grew angry.

I knew mother was busy making custards and cakes for Aunt Cordelia, and I longed to be in watching these pleasing operations. I thought—but what does it matter what I thought? I was bad! I was so bad that I was glad I was bad. Perhaps it was nerves. Maybe I really had taken care of the baby too long. But however that may be, for the first time in my life I enjoyed the consciousness of having a bad disposition—or perhaps I ought to say that I felt a fiendish satisfaction in the discovery that I had one.

Along in the middle of the afternoon three of the girls in the neighbourhood came over to play. They had their dolls, and they wanted to "keep house" in the "new part" of our home. We were living in a roomy and comfortable "addition," which had, oddly enough, been built before the building to which it was finally to serve as an annex. That is to say, it had been the addition before there was anything to add it to. By this time, however, the new house was getting a trifle old, as it waited for the completion of its rather disproportionate splendours; splendours which represented the ambitions rather than the achievements of the family. It towered, large, square, imposing, with hints of M. Mansard's grandiose architectural ideas in its style, in the very centre of a village block of land. From the first, it exercised a sort of "I dreamt I dwelt in marble halls" effect upon me, and in a vague way, at the back of my mind, floated the idea that when we passed from our modest home into this commanding edifice, well-trained servants mysteriously would appear, beautiful gowns would be found awaiting my use in the closets, and father and mother would be able to take their ease, something after the fashion of the "landed gentry" of whom I had read in Scotch and English books. The ceilings of the new house were so high, the sweep of the stairs so dramatic, the size of the drawing-rooms so copious, that perhaps I hardly was to be blamed for expecting a transformation scene.

But until this new life was realised, the clean, bare rooms made the best of all possible play-rooms, and with the light streaming in through the trees, and falling, delicately tinged with green, upon the new floors, and with the scent of the new wood all about, it was a place of indefinable enchantment. I was allowed to play there all I pleased—except when I had Julie. There were unguarded windows and yawning stair-holes, and no steps as yet leading from the ground to the great opening where the carved front door was some time to be. Instead, there were planks, inclined at a steep angle, beneath which lay the stones of which the foundation to the porch were to be made. Jagged pieces of yet unhewn sandstone they were, with cruel edges.

But to-day when the girls said, "Oh, come!" my newly discovered badness echoed their words. I wanted to go with them. So I went.

Out of the corner of my eye I could see father in the distance, but I wouldn't look at him for fear he would be magnetised into turning my way. The girls had gone up, and I followed, with Julie in my arms. Did I hear father call to me to stop? He always said I did, but I think he was mistaken. Perhaps I merely didn't wish to hear him. Anyway, I went on, balancing myself as best I could. The other girls had reached the top, and turned to look at us, and I knew they were afraid. I think they would have held out their hands to help me, but I had both arms clasped about Julie. So I staggered on, got almost to the top, then seemed submerged beneath a wave of fears—mine and those of the girls—and fell! As I went, I curled like a squirrel around Julie, and when I struck, she was still in my grasp and on top of me. But she rolled out of my relaxing clutch after that, and when father and mother came running, she was lying on the stones. They thought she had fallen that way, and as the breath had been fairly knocked out of her little body, so that she was not crying, they were more frightened than ever, and ran with her to the house, wild with apprehension.

As for me, I got up somehow and followed. I decided no bones were broken, but I was dizzy and faint, and aching from bruises. I saw my little friends running down the plank and making off along the poplar drive, white-faced and panting. I knew they thought Julie was dead and that I'd be hung. I had the same idea.

When we got to the sitting-room I had a strange feeling of never having seen it before. The tall stove, the green and oak ingrain car-pet, the green rep chairs, the what-not with its shells, the steel engravings on the walls, seemed absolutely strange. I sat down and counted the diamond-shaped figures on the oilcloth in front of the stove; and after a long time I heard Julie cry, and mother say with immeasurable relief:

"Aside from a shaking up, I don't believe she's a bit the worse."

Then some one brought me a cupful of cold water and asked me if I was hurt. I shook my head and would not speak. I then heard, in simple and emphatic Anglo-Saxon the opinions of my father and mother about a girl who would put her little sister's life in danger, and would disobey her parents. And after that I was put in my mother's bedroom to pass the rest of the day, and was told I needn't expect to come to the table with the others.

I accepted my fate stoically, and being permitted to carry my own chair into the room, I put it by the western window, which looked across two miles of meadows waving in buckwheat, in clover and grass, and sat there in a curious torpor of spirit. I was glad to be alone, for I had discovered a new idea — the idea of sin. I wished to be left to myself till I could think out what it meant. I believed I could do that by night, and, after I had got to the root of the matter, I could cast the whole ugly thing out of my soul and be good all the rest of my life.

There was a large upholstered chair standing in front of me, and I put my head down on the seat of that and thought and thought. My thoughts reached so far that I grew frightened, and I was relieved when I felt the little soft grey veils drawing about me which I knew meant sleep. It seemed to me that I really ought to weep — that the circumstances were such that I should weep. But sleep was sweeter than tears, and not only the pain in my mind but the jar and bruise of my body seemed to demand that oblivion. So I gave way to the impulse, and the grey veils wrapped around and around me as a spider's web enwraps a fly. And for hours I knew nothing.

When I awoke it was the close of day. Long tender shadows lay across the fields, the sky had that wonderful clearness and kindness which is like a human eye, and the soft wind puffing in at the window was sweet with field fragrance. A glass of milk and a plate with two slices of bread lay on the window sill by me, as if some one had placed them there from the outside. I could hear birds settling down for the night, and cheeping drowsily to each other. My cat came on the scene and, seeing me, looked at me with serious, expanding eyes, twitched her whiskers cynically, and passed on. Presently I heard the voices of my family. They were re-entering the sitting-room. Supper was over—supper, with its cold meats and shining jellies, its "floating island" and its fig cake. I could hear a voice that was new to me. It was deeper than my mother's, and its accent was different. It was the sort of a voice that made you feel that its owner had talked with many different kinds of people, and had contrived to hold her own with all of them. I knew it belonged to Aunt Cordelia. And now that I was not to see her, I felt my curiosity arising in me. I wanted to look at her, and still more I wished to ask her about goodness. She was rich and good! Was one the result of the other? And which came first? I dimly perceived that if there had been more money in our house there would have been more help, and I would not have been led into temptation—baby would not have been left too long upon my hands. However, after a few moments of self-pity, I rejected this thought. I knew I really was to blame, and it occurred to me that I would add to my faults if I tried to put the blame on anybody else.

Now that the first shock was over and that my sleep had refreshed me, I began to see what terrible sorrow had been mine if the fall had really injured Julie; and a sudden thought shook me. She might, after all, have been hurt in some way that would show itself later on. I yearned to look upon her, to see if all her sweetness and softness was intact. It seemed to me that if I could not see her the rising grief in me would break, and I would sob aloud. I didn't want to do that. I had no notion to call any attention to myself whatever, but see the baby I must. So, softly, and like a thief, I opened the door communicating with the little dressing-room in which Julie's cradle stood. The curtain had been drawn and it was almost dark, but I found my way to Julie's bassinet. I could not quite see her, but the delicate odour of her breath came up to me, and I found her little hand and slipped my finger in it. It was gripped in a baby pressure, and I stood there enraptured, feeling as if a flower had caressed me. I was thrilled through and through with happiness, and with love for this little creature, whom my selfishness might have destroyed. There was nothing in what had happened during this moment or two when I stood by her side to assure me that all was well with her; but I did so believe, and I said over and over: "Thank you, God! Thank you, God!"

And now my tears began to flow. They came in a storm—a storm I could not control, and I fled back to mother's room, and stood there before the west window weeping as I never had wept before.

The quiet loveliness of the closing day had passed into the splendour of the afterglow. Mighty wings as of bright angels, pink and shining white, reached up over the sky. The vault was purple above me, and paled to lilac, then to green of unimaginable tenderness. Now I quenched my tears to look, and then I wept again, weeping no more for sorrow and loneliness and shame than for gratitude and delight in beauty. So fair a world! What had sin to do with it? I could not make it out.

The shining wings grew paler, faded, then darkened; the melancholy sound of cow-bells stole up from the common. The birds were still; a low wind rustled the trees. I sat thinking my young "night thoughts" of how marvellous it was for the sun to set, to rise, to keep its place in heaven—of how wrapped about with mysteries we were. What if the world should start to falling through space? Where would it land? Was there even a bottom to the universe? "World without end" might mean that there was neither an end to space nor yet to time. I shivered at thought of such vastness.

Suddenly light streamed about me, warm arms enfolded me.

"Mother!" I murmured, and slipped from the unknown to the dear familiarity of her shoulder.

It was, I soon perceived, a silk-clad shoulder. Mother had on her best dress; nay, she wore her coral pin and ear-rings. Her lace collar was scented with Jockey Club, and her neck, into which I was burrowing, had the indescribable something that was not quite odour, not all softness, but was compounded of these and meant mother. She said little to me as she drew me away and bathed my face, brushed and plaited my hair, and put on my clean frock. But we felt happy together. I knew she was as glad to forgive as I was to be forgiven.

In a little while she led me, blinking, into the light. A tall stranger, a lady in prune-coloured silk, sat in the high-backed chair.

"This is my eldest girl, Aunt Cordelia," said my mother. I went forward timidly, wondering if I were really going to be greeted by this person who must have heard such terrible reports of me. I found myself caught by the hands and drawn into the embrace of this new, grand acquaintance.

"Well, I've been wanting to see you," said the rich, kind voice. "They say you look as I did at your age. They say you are like me!"

Like her—who was good! But no one referred to this difference or said anything about my sins. When we were sorry, was evil, then, forgotten and sin forgiven? A weight as of iron dropped from my spirit. I sank with a sigh on the hassock at my aunt's feet. I was once more a member of society.

VI. TRAVEL

IT was time to say good-bye.

I had been down to my little brother's grave and watered the sorrel that grew on it — I thought it was sorrow, and so tended it; and I had walked around the house and said good-bye to every window, and to the robin's nest, and to my playhouse in the shed. I had put a clean ribbon on the cat's neck, and kissed my doll, and given presents to my little sisters. Now, shivering beneath my new grey jacket in the chill of the May morning air, I stood ready to part with my mother. She was a little flurried with having just ironed my pinafores and collars, and with having put the last hook on my new Stuart plaid frock, and she looked me over with rather an anxious eye. As for me, I thought my clothes charming, and I loved the scarlet quill in my grey hat, and the set of my new shoes. I hoped, above all, that no one would notice that I was trembling and lay it down to fear.

Of course, I had been away before. It was not the first time I had left everything to take care of itself. But this time I was going alone, and that gave rather a different aspect to things. To go into the country for a few days, or even to Detroit, in the company of a watchful parent, might be called a "visit"; but to go alone, partly by train and partly by stage, and to arrive by one's self, amounted to "travel." I had an aunt who had travelled, and I felt this morning that love of travel ran in the family. Probably even Aunt Cordelia had been a trifle nervous, at first, when she started out for Hawaii, say, or for Egypt.

Mother and I were both fearful that the driver of the station 'bus hadn't really understood that he was to call. First she would ask father, and then I would ask him, if he was quite sure the man understood, and father said that if the man could understand English at all — and he supposed he could — he had understood that. Father was right about it, too, for just when we — that is, mother and I — were almost giving up, the 'bus horses swung in the big gate and came pounding up the drive between the Lombardy poplars, which were out in their yellow-green spring dress. They were a bay team with a yellow harness which clinked splendidly with bone rings, and the 'bus was as yellow as a pumpkin, and shaped not unlike one, so that I gave it my instant approval. It was precisely the sort of vehicle in which I would have chosen to go away. So absorbed was I in it that, though I must have kissed mother, I have really no recollection of it; and it was only when we were swinging out of the gate, and I looked back and saw her standing in the door watching us, that a terrible pang came over me, so that for one crazy moment I thought I was going to jump out and run back to her.

But I held on to father's hand and turned my face away from home with all the courage I could summon, and we went on through the town and out across a lonely stretch of country to the railroad. For we were an obstinate little town, and would not build up to the railroad because the railroad had refused to run up to us. It was a new station with a fine echo in it, and the man who called out the trains had a beautiful voice for echoes. It was created to inspire them and to encourage them, and I stood fascinated by the thunderous noises he was making till father seized me by the hand and thrust me into the care of the train conductor. They said something to each other in the sharp, explosive way men have, and the conductor took me to a seat and told me I was his girl for the time being, and to stay right there till he came for me at my station.

What amazed me was that the car should be full of people. I could not imagine where they all could be going. It was all very well for me, who belonged to a family of travellers—as witness Aunt Cordelia—to be going on a journey, but for these others, these many, many others, to be wandering around, heaven knows where, struck me as being not right. It seemed to take somewhat from the glory of my adventure.

However, I noticed that most of them looked poor. Their clothes were old and ugly; their faces not those of pleasure-seekers. It was very difficult to imagine that they could afford a journey, which was, as I believed, a great luxury. At first, the people looked to be all of a sort, but after a little I began to see the differences, and to notice that this one looked happy, and that one sad, and another as if he had much to do and liked it, and several others as if they had very little idea where they were going or why.

But I liked better to look from the windows and to see the world. The houses seemed quite familiar and as if I had seen them often before. I hardly could believe that I hadn't walked up those paths, opened those doors and seated myself at the tables. I felt that if I went in those houses I would know where everything was—just where the dishes were kept, and the Bible, and the jam. It struck me that houses were very much alike in the world, and that led to the thought that people, too, were probably alike. So I forgot what the conductor had said to me about keeping still, and I crossed over the aisle and sat down beside a little girl who was regrettably young, but who looked pleasant. Her mother and grandmother were sitting opposite, and they smiled at me in a watery sort of way as if they thought a smile was expected of them. I meant to talk to the little girl, but I saw she was almost on the verge of tears, and it didn't take me long to discover what was the matter. Her little pink hat was held on by an elastic band, which, being put behind her ears and under her chin, was cutting her cruelly. I knew by experience that if the band were placed in front of her ears the tension would be lessened; so, with the most benevolent intentions in the world, I inserted my fingers between the rubber and her chubby cheeks, drew it out with nervous but friendly fingers, somehow let go of it, and snap across her two red cheeks and her pretty pug nose went the lacerating elastic, leaving a welt behind it!

"What do you mean, you bad girl?" cried the mother, taking me by the shoulders with a sort of grip I had never felt before. "I never saw such a child—never!"

An old woman with a face like a hen leaned over the back of the seat.

"What's she done? What's she done?" she demanded. The mother told her, as the grandmother comforted the hurt baby.

"Go back to your seat and stay there!" commanded the mother. "See you don't come near here again!"

My lips trembled with the anguish I could hardly restrain. Never had a noble soul been more misunderstood. Stupid beings! How dare they! Yet, not to be liked by them—not to be understood! That was unendurable. Would they listen to the gentle word that turneth away wrath? I was inclined to think not. I was fairly panting under my load of dismay and despondency, when a large man with an extraordinarily clean appearance sat down opposite me. He was a study in grey—grey suit, tie, socks, gloves, hat, top-coat—yes, and eyes! He leaned forward ingratiatingly.

"What do you think Aunt Ellen sent me last week?" he inquired.

We seemed to be old acquaintances, and in my second of perplexity I decided that it was mere forgetfulness that made me unable to recall just whom he was talking about. So I only said politely: "I don't know, I'm sure, sir."

"Why, yes, you do!" he laughed. "Couldn't you guess? What should Aunt Ellen send but some of that white maple sugar of hers; better than ever, too. I've a pound of it along with me, and I'd be glad to pry off a few pieces if you'd like to eat it. You always were so fond of Aunt Ellen's maple sugar, you know."

The tone carried conviction. Of course I must have been fond of it; indeed, upon reflection, I felt that I had been. By the time the man was back with a parallelogram of the maple sugar in his hand, I was convinced that he had spoken the truth.

"Aunt Ellen certainly is a dear," he went on. "I run down to see her every time I get a chance. Same old rain-barrel! Same old bee-hives! Same old well-sweep! Wouldn't trade them for any others in the world. I like everything about the place—like the 'Old Man' that grows by the gate; and the tomato trellis—nobody else treats tomatoes like flowers; and the herb garden, and the cupboard with the little wood-carvings in it that Uncle Ben made. You remember Uncle Ben? Been a sailor—broke both legs—had 'em cut off—and sat around and carved while Aunt Ellen taught school. Happy they were—no one happier. Brought me up, you know. Didn't have a father or mother—just gathered me in. Good sort, those. Uncle Ben's gone, but Aunt Ellen's a mother to me yet. Thinks of me, travelling, travelling, never putting my head down in the same bed two nights running; and here and there and everywhere she overtakes me with little scraps out of home. That's Aunt Ellen for you!"

As the delicious sugar melted on my tongue, the sorrows melted in my soul, and I was just about to make some inquiries about Aunt Ellen, whose personal qualities seemed to be growing clearer and clearer in my mind, when my conductor came striding down the aisle.

"Where's my little girl?" he demanded heartily. "Ah, there she is, just where I left her, in good company and eating maple sugar, as I live."

"Well, she hain't bin there all the time now, I ken tell ye that!" cried the old woman with a face like a hen.

"Indeed, she ain't!" the other women joined in. "She's a mischief-makin' child, that's what she is!" said the mother. The little girl was looking over her grandmother's shoulder, and she ran out a very red, serpent-like tongue at me.

"She's a good girl, and almost as fond of Aunt Ellen as I am," said the large man, finding my pocket, and putting a huge piece of maple sugar in it.

The conductor, meantime, was gathering my things, and with a "Come along, now! This is where you change," he led me from the car. I glanced back once, and the hen-faced woman shook her withered brown fist at me, and the large man waved and smiled. The conductor and I ran as hard as we could, he carrying my light luggage, to a stage that seemed to be waiting for us. He shouted some directions to the driver, deposited me within, and ran back to his train. And I, alone again, looked about me.

We were in the heart of a little town, and a number of men were standing around while the horses took their fill at the watering-trough. This accomplished, the driver checked up the horses, mounted to his high seat, was joined by a heavy young man; two gentlemen entered the inside of the coach, and we were off.

One of these gentlemen was very old. His silver hair hung on his shoulders; he had a beautiful flowing heard which gleamed in the light, the kindest of faces, lit with laughing blue eyes, and he leaned forward on his heavy stick and seemed to mind the plunging of our vehicle. The other man was middle-aged, dark, silent-looking, and, I decided, rather like a king. We all rode in silence for a while, but by and by the old man said kindly:

"Where are you going, my child?"

I told him.

"And whose daughter are you?" he inquired. I told him that with pride. "I know people all through the state," he said, "but I don't seem to remember that name."

"Don't you remember my father, sir?" I cried, anxiously, edging up closer to him. "Not that great and good man! Why, Abraham Lincoln and my father are the greatest men that ever lived!"

His head nodded strangely, as he lifted it and looked at me with his laughing eye.

"It's a pity I don't know him, that being the case," he said gently. "But, anyway, you're a lucky little girl."

"Yes," I sighed, "I am, indeed."

But my attention was taken by our approach to what I recognised as an "estate." A great gate with high posts, flat on top, met my gaze, and through this gateway I could see a drive and many beautiful trees. A little boy was sitting on top of one of the posts, watching us, and I thought I never had seen a place better adapted to viewing the passing procession. I longed to be on the other gate-post, exchanging confidences across the harmless gulf with this nice-looking boy, when, most unexpectedly, the horses began to plunge. The next second the air was filled with buzzing black objects.

"Bees!" said the king. It was the first word he had spoken, and a true word it was. Swarming bees had settled in the road, and we had driven unaware into the midst of them. The horses were distracted, and made blindly for the gate, though they seemed much more likely to run into the posts than to get through the gate, I thought. The boy seemed to think this, too, for he shot backward, turned a somersault in the air, and disappeared from view.

"God bless me!" said the king.

The heavy young man on the front seat jumped from his place and began beating away the bees and holding the horses by the bridles, and in a few minutes we were on our way. The horses had been badly stung, and the heavy young man looked rather bumpy.

As for us, the king had shut the stage door at the first approach of trouble, and we were unharmed.

After this, we all felt quite well acquainted, and the old gentleman told me some wonderful stories about going about among the Indians and about the men in the lumber camps and the settlers on the lake islands. Afterward I learned that he was a bishop, and a brave and holy man whom it was a great honour to meet, but, at the time, I only thought of how kind he was to pare apples for me and to tell me tales. The king seldom spoke more than one word at a time, but he was kind, too, in his way. Once he said, "Sleepy?" to me. And, again, "Hungry?" He didn't look out at the landscape at all, and neither did the bishop. But I ran from one side to the other, and the last of the journey I was taken up between the driver and the heavy man on the high seat.

Presently we were in a little town with cottages almost hidden among the trees. A blue stream ran through green fields, and the water dashed over a dam. I could hear the song of the mill and the ripping of the boards.

"We're here!" said the driver.

The heavy man lifted me down, and my young uncle came running out with his arms open to receive me. "What a traveller!" he said, kissing me.

"It's been a tremendously long and interesting journey," I said.

"Yes," he answered. "Ten miles by rail and ten by stage. I suppose you've had a great many adventures!"

"Oh, yes!" I cried, and ached to tell them, but feared this was not the place. I saw my uncle respectfully helping the bishop to alight, and heard him inquiring for his health, and the bishop answering in his kind, deep voice, and saying I was indeed a good traveller and saw all there was to see—and a little more. The king shook hands with me, and this time said two words: "Good luck." Uncle had no idea who he was—no one had seen him before. Uncle didn't quite like his looks. But I did. He was uncommon; he was different. I thought of all those people in the train who had been so alike. And then I remembered what unexpected differences they had shown, and turned to smile at my uncle.

"I should say I have had adventures!" I cried.

"We'll get home to your aunt," he said, "and then we'll hear all about them."

We crossed a bridge above the roaring mill-race, went up a lane, and entered Arcadia. That was the way it seemed to me. It was really a cottage above a stream, where youth and love dwelt, and honour and hospitality, and the little house was to be exchanged for a greater one where—though youth departed—love and honour and hospitality were still to dwell.

"Travel's a great thing," said my uncle, as he helped me off with my jacket.

"Yes," I answered, solemnly, "it is a great privilege to see the world."

I still am of that opinion. I have seen some odd bits of it, and I cannot understand why it is that other journeys have not quite come up to that first one, when I heard of Aunt Ellen, and saw the boy turn the surprised somersault, and was welcomed by two lovers in a little Arcadia.